The New Baby Calf

To Cassidy
Merry Christmas
From 2005!
& Mrs. Martin

Scholastic Canada Ltd.
175 Hillmount Road, Markham, Ontario, Canada L6C 1Z7

Scholastic Inc.
555 Broadway, New York, NY 10012, USA

Scholastic Australia Pty Limited
PO Box 579, Gosford, NSW 2250, Australia

Scholastic New Zealand Limited
Private Bag 94407, Greenmount, Auckland, New Zealand

Scholastic Ltd.
Villiers House, Clarendon Avenue, Leamington Spa,
Warwickshire CV32 5PR, UK

Photography by Ian Crysler
Cover photo of Barbara Reid by Ian Crysler

12 11 10 9 8   Printed in Canada   3 4 5 / 0

Canadian Cataloguing in Publication Data

Chase, Edith Newlin
The new baby calf

ISBN 0-590-73678-7

1. Calves—Juvenile poetry. I. Reid, Barbara, 1957-
II. Title.

PZ8.3.C358Ne 1990   j811'.54   C90-094419-0

The New Baby Calf

EDITH NEWLIN CHASE BARBARA REID

SCHOLASTIC CANADA

Toronto • Sydney • New York • London • Auckland

Buttercup the cow had
a new baby calf,
a fine baby calf,
a strong baby calf.

Not strong like his mother,
but strong for a calf,
for this baby calf was so new.

Buttercup licked him
with her strong warm tongue.

Buttercup washed him
with her strong warm tongue.

Buttercup brushed him
with her strong warm tongue.

And the new baby calf liked that!

The new baby calf took
a very little walk,
a teeny little walk,
a tiny little walk.

His skinny legs wobbled
when he took that little walk,
and the new baby calf fell down.

Buttercup told him
with a soft, low "Moo-oo!"
that he was doing well
for one so very new.
She talked very gently,
as mother cows do.

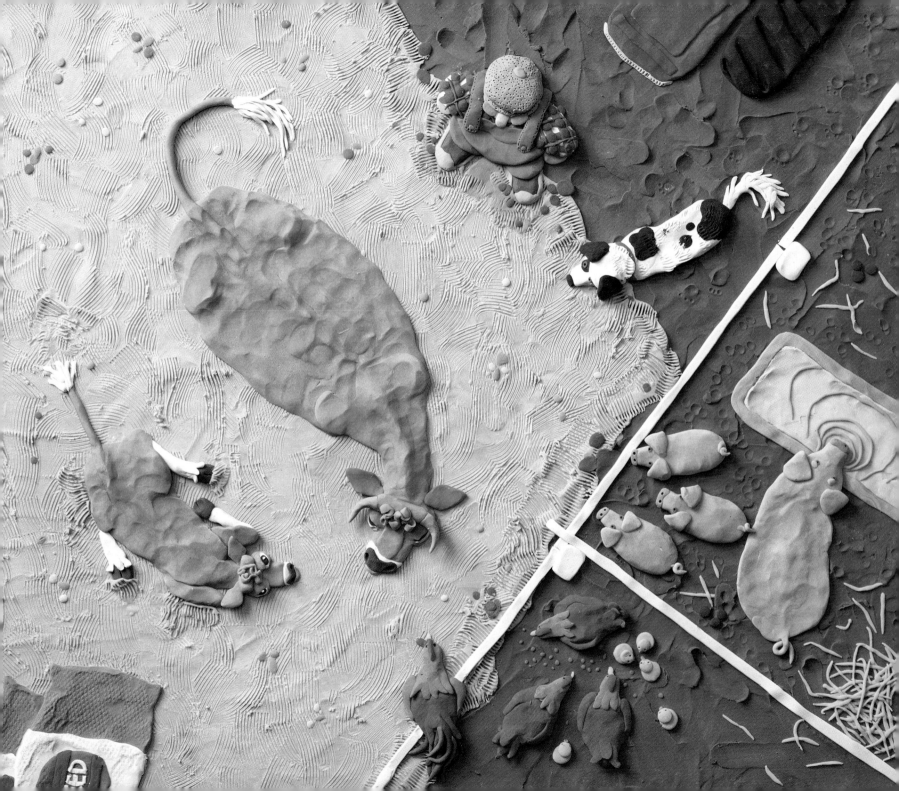

And the new baby calf liked that!

The new baby calf took
another little walk,
a little longer walk,
a little stronger walk.

He walked around his mother
and he found a place to drink.
And the new baby calf liked that!

Buttercup told him
with another low "Moo-oo!"
that drinking milk from mother
was a fine thing to do.
She had enough for him,
and for the farmer too.

And the new baby calf liked that!

The new baby calf

drank from mother every day.

His legs grew strong

so he could run and kick and play.

He began to eat grass,

and lots of grain and hay.

And the big baby calf grew fat!